First published in Japan in 1988 by Shiko-Sha Co., Ltd., Tokyo,
under the title *Mori No Akachan.*
Published in the United States, Great Britain, Canada, Australia, and New Zealand in
2009 by North-South Books Inc.,
an imprint of NordSüd Verlag AG, Zürich, Switzerland.
Distributed in the United States by North-South Books Inc., New York.

Library of Congress Cataloging-in-Publication Data is available.
ISBN 978-0-7358-2228-3 (trade edition)
Printed in China by Colorprint Offset (Shenzhen) Co. Ltd., Shenzhen, P.R.C., December 2009
3 5 7 9 • 10 8 6 4 2

www.northsouth.com

Kazuo Iwamura

HOORAY for SPRING!

NorthSouth
New York / London

Spring was here at last!

Mick, Mack, and Molly leaped from branch to branch.

"Hooray for spring!" they shouted.

"Look!" called Mack. "Caterpillars!
They're eating the leaves."

"That's what caterpillars like to eat,"
Molly explained.

"Look at the beautiful cherry blossoms!" said Molly.

"And the bees!" Mick shouted.

"They are sucking the nectar from the blossoms," Molly explained.

"Look!" said Mack. "A baby bird!
Is it lost? It looks hungry."
    "What do baby birds like to eat?"
asked Mick.
    "I don't know," said Molly.

"Maybe pine-cones," said Mick.
"Yummy," said Mack.
"I don't think so," said Molly.

"Here, baby bird," said Mick.

"We brought you some pine-cones."

"The seeds are delicious!" said Mack.

But the baby bird shook its head.

It did not want any pine-cones.

"That's what I thought," said Molly.

"How about some sweet cherry blossoms?" said Molly.

"The bees love them," said Mack.

"I don't think baby birds do," said Mick.

"Here, baby bird," said Molly. "Have some cherry blossoms. The bees make honey with them."

But the baby bird shook its head again. It even shook its little wings. It did not want any cherry blossoms.

"I thought so," said Mick.

"What does this baby eat?" said Mick.

"Acorns?" suggested Mack.

"Raspberries?" suggested Molly. "Mushrooms?
Walnuts? Milk?"

"That's right! Milk from its mama!"
shouted Mick.

And then . . .

. . . up flew Mama bird—with a fat green worm
in her mouth!

The baby bird raised its head happily. It opened
its mouth wide. And . . .

. . . in went the worm!
Delicious!

"You should have seen the baby bird,"
Mick told Mama and Papa.

"It didn't want pine-cones for lunch,"
said Molly.

"Or cherry blossoms," said Mick.

"It wanted a worm!" said Molly.

"The baby opened its mouth, and in it went,"
said Mick.

"Look!" said Mack. "I'm a baby bird!"

And everybody laughed.